# WAITING FOR NERUDA'S MEMOIRS

*laura boggess*

*the poetry club series*

*ts* T. S. Poetry Press • New York

T. S. Poetry Press
Briarcliff, New York
Tspoetry.com
© 2020 by Laura Boggess

Cover image by L.L. Barkat

Kool-Aid, a brand mentioned in this text, is owned by Kraft Heinz.

ISBN 978-1-943120-44-4


Cataloging-in-Publication Data:
Boggess, Laura
        [Fiction.]
        Waiting for Neruda's Memoirs.
            The poetry club series/Laura Boggess
        ISBN 978-1-943120-44-4

She stared up at the ceiling as he studied the paper. Swung her feet back and forth under the desk. She could barely reach the gleaming tile floor with her tiptoes. Who made these chairs anyway? The Jolly Green Giant?

She tried breathing deeply…slowly and quietly gulping up the atmosphere. But something about the way he raised his eyebrow as he read niggled. She knew what was coming.

The voices of the watchers hissed in her ear. *Who does he think he is? That he could sit there and read about you—about you, for heaven's sake—without saying one word? As if you weren't sitting there right in front of him. And now this: A raised eyebrow?*

She tried ignoring the voice. But the more she resisted, the more insistent it grew—dividing into multiple echoes until a cacophony filled her head. Panic welled inside her as the voices reached a crescendo. She glanced frantically at the man studying her resume.

"Those aren't the best pieces of me, you know."

As soon as she spoke, the voices quieted and she felt immediate gratitude.

He lifted his eyes and looked at her over his glasses—eyebrows raised again.

"Pardon me?"

"Those aren't the best pieces of me."

He looked absolutely baffled.

"I'm sorry, I'm afraid I don't know what you mean."

"Well, you can't expect me to bring the best parts, can you?

Not to a perfect stranger. Not to someone I don't even know."

His mouth was hanging open now and he dropped the resume on his desk in front of him.

"I'm sorry...I don't..."

She was feeling quite indignant and the watchers' pleasure heated up her cheeks. But just as quickly as the triumph *umphed*, the reality of the situation dropped hard between them. Amy looked at the bank manager looking at her. He wasn't much older than she—probably mid-forties. He had taken his suit jacket off when they entered his office and as she walked through the door behind him she noticed that his white shirt was terribly wrinkled in the back—he had only pressed the front. A practical man. How could he possibly understand?

And yet...he had been kind to her—had smiled with his whole face—even his eyes. If he noticed her dress was too large, he hadn't let on—as if he frequently interviewed malnourished neurotic women. He had inquired about her life with genuine interest—was she from around here? What brought her to these parts of Virginia?

Now, he stared openly at her with the expression of someone who had just discovered mold on a piece of bread already half eaten. She watched as the slightly shocked expression faded into one of concern. He leaned closer to her over the top of his desk.

"Ms. Pinkleberry...are you okay?"

He knit his brows together and slid his hand across the desk tentatively, his fingers stopping just short of hers. As if bridging the distance between them might bring her to her senses. The kindness was more than she could bear.

"Oh, nevermind!"

She stood up abruptly as tears welled, grabbed the resume from his desk, and fled the office. She didn't stop running until she was two blocks away…then she leaned up against a gray brick office building and sobbed uncontrollably.

So. Steven was right. She really was crazy.

*She needed that poetry book.*

Amy stared out the window at her empty mailbox. A few frail flakes skitted in the rushing currents. Thirty-mile-an-hour wind gusts, the radio said. She watched her neighbor's garbage can pick up speed as it rolled down the street.

*I should be nice and go get that.*

Then: a loud crashing noise from the back deck. She would have to break the vigil. More rumbling and tumbling sounds greeted her as she approached the back doors, mustering the ability to care. One quick peek through the glass, however, lent her the required urgency. As soon as she opened the door the wind plucked it from her fingers, slamming it against the condo's siding.

*Why didn't I put this stuff in storage?*

The deck furniture had taken flight. The umbrella—neatly rolled up and tied—had nevertheless served as sail to the patio table, and now the two hung like Siamese twins, dangling over the deck rail. When she stepped forward to rescue the twins, a chair came sliding toward her. She sidestepped, grabbed her attacker by the arms from behind and wrangled the thing through the door. Five more chairs and the set of twins later, Amy sat panting on her living room floor. Her slippers were soaking wet and the wind had cut cold straight through to her bones. She stared out the French doors at the snow falling down and burst into tears.

*You're never going to make it.*

The watchers were back. After Steven left, the voices stopped for a time. Dr. Larinsky thought it was due to the new medication. Amy did too. And then winter came.

*You'll never make it on your own. You can't even find a job. The money he gave you is about to run out. How will you pay for this place? How will you survive? You might as well give up now. Just do it. Quit. Quit this thing. There's no use trying.*

"Shut up!"

But they refused to be quiet—watching her every move, berating her every action and decision for the past ten years until she was curled up on the floor—a quivering, tearful mess. She must have fallen asleep, because when she opened her eyes it was dark outside. She straightened her body and let the cold of the wood floor melt through her PJs and into her skin. She listened to the wind continue its wreckage outside. The cold of the floor made her tingle, awakening forgotten nerve endings and calling them to move.

*You'll never make it.*

She buried her face in her hands, heaved a sigh and tried to wipe it all away.

*Just let that thought float by like a boat passing you on the river, Amy.*

She took three deep breaths with her eyes closed and on the third exhale rose to her feet. She peered through the glass doors, flicked on the deck light, and surveyed the damage. All of her terra cotta pots had been tipped, little piles of dirt now swirling atop remnants of snow. The railing had been knocked loose by the weight of the table, and she would have to repaint the white boards that the splintering planters had gouged.

And her living room was full of deck furniture.

She reached into the yawning mailbox and felt around deep inside. Nothing. Where could it be? She had been waiting for *Neruda's Memoirs* for two weeks. Usually, Amazon only took three days to get her order to her. *She needed that book.*

Poetry was the only thing that stopped the voices.

And not just any poetry. It had to be Maureen's. Her doctor called it obsessive-compulsive traits. Once she set her mind on something, nothing else would do. Last year it was Emily Dickinson. Steven had told her to take a class. *Do something with your life*, he had said. It was just on a whim that she signed up for the American Lit class at the campus downtown. Just to make him happy. She'd always loved poetry, but never felt it was practical. There weren't very many literature courses in the business track she took as a young co-ed. And later, when she was working on her MBA, there wasn't time for things like that. She'd worked a full-time administrative job and taken business classes in the evening. It was what was necessary to get Steven through medical school. The plan was, she would run his office when he started his OB/GYN practice. That's what she did too. For ten years. But…Steven had said *find something you love, for Pete's sake*. It was after they decided to stop with the in vitro—after she had descended as deep as she'd ever been in the blackness. Poetry was the only thing that made sense. And Dickinson?

> *Tell all the Truth but tell it slant—*
> *Success in Circuit lies…*

The first time she read it, she read her life. *Tell it slant.* Wasn't this how it had always been for her?

Amy shivered and walked stiffly back inside, securing the door against the wind behind her.

Steven was afraid of the voices. For as long as she could remember, the voices had been her constant companion. But when she was younger, they weren't quite so real…they weren't quite so loud.

As she grew older, they became more powerful. Dr. Larinsky called them auditory hallucinations. But Amy wasn't so sure. If they were, how could poetry make them go away? How could Emily Dickinson speak them into silence?

And now, it was Maureen Doallas. She had followed Maureen's blog for over a year—gobbling up every bit of poetry the woman laid down. Her work was simply brilliant. It was smart and fluid and echoed with deep loss and the incomparable joy of transcending it. When Amy had heard there was a book coming out, she was ecstatic. That was when Dickinson had stopped working.

*She needed that poetry book.*

Suddenly, it occurred to her. She could get online and track the order.

Shedding her shoes in steps, she ran to the living room couch—her makeshift office. She pulled her laptop out from under the sofa and unfolded it into her lap.

"Come on, come on."

The two-minute bootup never seemed so long. *Finally!* She pulled up her favorites and clicked on the Amazon link.

"There it is: Track your order."

It took some clicking around but she finally found it.

"Delivered!"

How could that be? There was no way she could have missed it. She'd been holding vigil for days. Ever since that dreadful bank interview.

At the memory of her most recent failure, Amy was flooded with self-loathing. But before it could find a voice her eyes landed on the problem.

*Delivered to: 108 Taylor Drive.*

Why, that wasn't her address! That was the house down the street. The big one, with the gate that closed and locked at night.

Well. Gate or no gate, she needed that book. Amy grabbed her puffy down coat, plunged her feet into the clogs she'd abandoned in the kitchen, and headed out into the wind and down the street.

The gate was open. Just a little.

Even the watchers were scared into silence as Amy gingerly pushed the big iron structure open just enough so she could squeeze through. Once inside, however, she was seized with sudden uncertainty. The house was not as large as she'd expected. It was only one story, for starters—a pale brick that seemed to wind around the property. The landscaping was immaculate. There was a ramp that curved around from the side of the house.

She looked up and waited for the watchers to tell her what to do. The wind had died down, leaving a gentle breeze that tickled her skin. Not a cloud in the sky and the words tumbled about in her head–

> *A sky dyed*
> *deep in indigo…*

A line from one of Maureen's poems she had read on her blog that morning.

*She needed that book.*

Sighing heavily, Amy marched forward. She climbed the steps determinedly, but before she could put finger to bell, the door opened.

"Oh, good, you're here. Follow me."

The girl couldn't have been more than ten years old. Her heart-shaped face and blonde ringlets were shockingly cute. But right now she was moving quickly and there seemed to be some sense of urgency. Amy ducked through the door and followed the girl, quickening her pace to match.

"She's been sleeping in the Great Room for a couple weeks now. It was the only place we could fit the hospital bed. It's worked out good, though; there's a full bath right close, and here she has all her books she loves."

As she talked, they entered a large, circular room. The ceiling arched up into a glass dome and sunlight cascaded down, coloring everything in golden hues. The circular walls were ensconced with shelves and Amy felt dizzy as she turned in place to take in all the books. She recognized this giddy, lifting feeling. This was how she had felt the first time she visited the library as a girl. Paradise.

Her gaze circled round until it landed on a peculiar sight. At the far arc was a hospital bed and in the bed was a very small, very old, very angry woman. Her white hair was carefully coiffed and lipstick amply applied. She sat bolt upright, arms crossed and steely eyes fixed defiantly on Amy.

Amy was bemused. Just then she noticed the small red and black book on a table beside the hospital bed. She could only just make out the sensuous colors of Randall David Tipton's "The Assumption of the Virgin" in the middle of the cover. Without thinking, she moved forward.

"Granny, this is your new nurse, " the little girl was saying. "Now you be nice to her! Dad had a lot of trouble convincing the company to send another…"

The elderly woman was watching Amy approach. *Say something,* the watchers said, but she couldn't seem to form the words. She had her eye on that book and that was all that mattered. She had found it. It was hers. She would take it and go home. It was that simple.

*Say something*, the watchers repeated.

"I'm sorry, but you are mistaken. " She nodded at the little girl and offered a quivering smile to the old woman. "I live up the street and just came to collect my book. It seems it was delivered here by mistake."

She reached out a shaky hand to pluck the book from the table.

But the old woman beat her to it. Before Amy knew what had happened, skinny fingers had grabbed *Neruda's Memoirs* right out from under hers.

Amy looked up in disbelief. The old woman had the book pressed to her emaciated chest, holding it in both hands like a prayer. The scowl on her face had disappeared and there was fear in her eyes. Amy watched as she struggled for composure.

"I—I…well, you must be Amelia."

She gave Amy a watery smile. The way the woman said her given name awoke a memory deep inside Amy's body and she felt herself responding physically to this frail creature. She began to relax.

"My name is Justine, " the woman smiled again. "I fear I owe you an apology…Alice opened the package by mistake and before we could return the book to you, I sort of…well, I fell right into it."

She laughed nervously and glanced at Amy.

"Yes, yes, I understand. Maureen Doallas writes beautifully, doesn't she? Now if you don't mind…"

Amy reached out her hand to receive the book.

But Justine continued to clutch those bound pages and her eyes filled with tears.

"It's just that…" she lowered her voice and locked eyes with Amy. "These words are the only thing that makes the pain stop."

This sudden admission took Amy aback, but before she could respond, a voice boomed down the hall.

"What is the gate doing open? Alice, how many times do I have to tell you to make sure it latches when…"

He stopped speaking when he saw Amy. Amy felt her knees grow weak as his eyes burned into her.

"Miss Pinkleberry, " he said. "What are you doing here?"

She thought she would never see him again. But now she was standing in his house. The bank manager she had fled from last week was her neighbor.

Shame burned her cheeks as she remembered their last encounter at the interview.

All eyes were on her and Amy wanted to run. The watchers began their laughter and she felt her defenses start the slow rise.

"What are you doing here, Ms. Pinkleberry?" He asked again.

"I-I came to get my book, " she said, hotly.

She turned to Justine, intending to forcefully remove the manuscript from the woman's hands if necessary. Those milky eyes were studying her intently and Amy saw comprehension dawn on the old woman's face. Slowly, Justine unwound her hands from her chest and held the book out to Amy.

Amy didn't know why she felt so guilty all of a sudden. *The book belonged to her, right?* But Justine's arms were so skinny…and her hands shook as she offered the book. Amy took it gently—and Justine's fingers only clung for a second.

"Thank you, " she said, softly. "I'll just be going now."

But as she turned to go Justine's voice followed her.

"Amelia?"

There it was again. That tugging. The way the old woman said her given name stirred memory. She turned around.

"Yes?"

"I am wondering…would you like a job? Just a couple hours a day, mind you. My nurse just quit on me and we have been unsuccessful in finding another and…"

"Justine!"

Color was rising in the man's face. Amy had never seen quite that shade of purple.

"It's true, Oliver, you can't keep coming home every two hours to check on me! Alice should not have to bear this…"

The man named Oliver turned to the little girl.

"Alice, would you please take Ms. Pinkleberry to the galley and find our guest something to drink? Your grandmother and I need to talk."

Amy shook her head and was about to refuse but the girl grabbed her hand and almost skipped her out of the room— through a swinging door with a circular glass window. They entered a long narrow kitchen with a raised bar down the center. The room was all shiny metallic and Amy was reminded of a fifties malt shop.

"I just made some orange Kool-Aid this morning!"

Amy started to respond but voices drifted through the swinging door—agitated voices of the two adults they left behind.

"Justine, are you out of your mind? You don't know anything about this woman!"

"I know she recognizes good poetry when she sees it and that's a darn sight better than these bobble-headed girls you have paraded through here these months…"

"Those girls were trained to take care of people. This girl has an MBA from Stanford! What in the world makes you think…Besides, she seems a bit…"

But Amy missed the last word because Alice started giggling.

"I love your socks."

Amy looked down. In her haste to get to *Neruda's Memoirs* she hadn't even considered her appearance. To her horror she saw that she hadn't even managed to match up her socks—one brightly colored striped variety paired with yellow and green polka dots. To make matters worse, her pajama bottoms were haphazardly tucked down in the things, giving her legs a clown-like appearance.

She smiled weakly at Alice.

"Thank you."

She readjusted the bottoms, shifting them over the brightly colored socks.

Alice opened the refrigerator door, talking all the while.

"We have the orange Kool-Aid, there's some soda in here, and Justine's tomato juice. What's yer poison?"

She dimpled just so that Amy was speechless for a second.

"Oh—um…I'm not really thirsty. And I really need to get back."

Amy clutched *Neruda's Memoirs* to her chest and made a movement to go.

"Wait!"

Amy sighed. Would she never escape?

"Don't you want to hear Gram's offer? We really do need someone to help. Someone…" she groped around for the right word. "Someone that Gram likes."

Such a solemn tone from so young a girl pulled at Amy's heart. Despite her anxiety, she wondered about Alice's story. Where was her mother? Why wasn't she in school? And what was wrong with her grandmother?

Amy sat down on one of the bar stools and bellied up to the counter.

"I'd love some tomato juice, please."

Alice smiled wide. She pulled a glass jar from the fridge.

"It wouldn't be for very long, you know. Dad says Gram is not long for this world. Her time is coming soon, he says. He just wants me to be prepared, he says. It's always been just the three of us. And I don't know what I'll do without Gram. But she's been sick for so long now. Dad says we should be glad when she's not suffering…"

The girl bubbled on, barely taking a breath between words. Amy felt dizzy.

"Alice. I haven't said yes. It sounds to me like your father does not want to hire me. I don't want to cause any problems. Besides…I've been looking for a *real* job."

She took a sip of the thick red juice the child placed before her. Alice climbed onto the stool beside hers and leaned elbows on the counter.

"Don't worry. Gram always gets what she wants. Dad talks a lot, but in the end, it's Gram who figures everything out."

Just then the door opened and a dark head peeked through.

"Ms. Pinkleberry? Would you mind coming back in here for a moment?"

Amy slid off the stool and pushed through the swinging door once again.

Justine sat upright in the hospital bed, cheeks flushed. There was a sparkle in her eye that was not there before. Triumph.

Amy couldn't help smiling at the accuracy of Alice's prediction.

"Ms. Pinkleberry, I know…" Oliver began.

"Amelia, " Justine interrupted. "When can you start? I just need three hours a day. The home health nurse will come for the hard parts. All that I want you to do is read to me. Are you interested?"

The watcher's started.

…*Stupidest thing I've ever heard…You can't get a real job…You can't make it on three hours a week…*

"I'm not sure…I've been looking for a job—full-time, with benefits…"

"Why don't we agree that you'll work for me until you find one?"

*What could it hurt?* Amy hesitated. Justine saw her chance.

"Come tomorrow at ten. You will lunch with us. Oliver will discuss pay."

She yawned.

"And now, I'm so sorry, dear, but I must get some rest. Oliver, will you show Amelia to the door?"

"Yes, of course. Just follow me."

He turned and headed toward the front hall. Amy followed his wrinkled back through the yawning archway.

"Amelia?"

Amy turned.

"Yes?"

"Bring *Neruda's Memoirs* with you tomorrow, will you?"

Amy sank her teeth into the airy white bread and the tangy sweetness of grape jelly melted into her tongue. She swung her legs back and forth under the table. The old lady was talking and she was trying to listen, but that purple goodness was gooping out the sides of the bread, forcing her to tilt her head to catch it. And her own memories were flooding in.

Amy had cried a lot at first—so much she hadn't wanted to eat. The missing of her momma was more than she could stand. And her daddy too. And when her grandma came to stay with her, she thought it only temporary. That they would be coming home soon. She thought that all the way through the funerals and up until the grandmother told her that her mommy and daddy were in heaven.

*What was Justine saying now?* The silver head was bending close. Those slender fingers with the bunchy skin were wrapping around hers. Milk-blue eyes sought her own.

"You're going to be okay, Amelia. We're going to take care of each other. It's just you and me now."

*Just you and me now.*

Steven had once told her that too.

*They always go away.*

The watchers hissed in her ear.

Amy awoke with a start. She slapped the alarm into submission and stared at the ceiling. She resisted the urge to turn to the empty side of the bed. She must face these things alone now.

But her Gran's face seemed so real. And for a minute she

was four years old again…waiting for momma and daddy. She closed her eyes and tried to remember their faces. All she could conjure was the snapshot taken on their wedding day that she had tucked away in the safe in the closet in the second bedroom.

But Gran's face? That was another story. She closed her eyes and brought the dream to mind—she knew every curve of that woman's mouth…every wrinkle on her brow. And her eyes—how they could speak the mischief of her mind.

The sobs that wracked her small frame now took her by surprise. Blindly, she fumbled for the book on the table. Drew it like air to parched lungs. It fell open to page ninety-five.

> *Pain isn't a wound*
> *we can stitch*
> *to a close…*

She let her eyes linger over the rest of the poem until her heart slowed and her breathing smoothed. This one said so much. "Heartfelt," it was called. *It was.*

Amy had read it over and over last night before giving in to sleep. Somehow, Maureen Doallas's words had become her lullaby.

She looked at the clock. Only an hour before it was time to read to Justine. As she put her feet to the floor, she carried the last lines of the poem with her.

> *Measure pain slowly,*
> *wait for it to dull,*
> *offer it time and memory.*

She hadn't meant to stay so long.

Every day this week it was the same: two poems a day and Justine asleep in half an hour. Amy obediently sat beside the sleeping woman for two-and-a-half more hours...just in case. Alice was "in the library" having her lessons. Amy never saw the girl—until today.

Justine had only wanted one poem today. Amy read "A Mother-To-Be in Waiting."

*In the space between*
*the waiting*
*and the coming*

*there is moonlight*
*given to morning*

*Breaths held*
*released*
*now holding*

*soon seek*
*to give light*
*to give life*
*to give love*

After the reading both women were affected. Amy was left wondering if this is what it was like to hold a child of one's own—*is it holding moonlight in your arms?* The ache in her womb and her empty arms throbbed. Justine turned her face away and grew silent.

"Justine?"

The old woman turned doleful eyes back to Amy.

"I'm sorry, Amelia. Those last lines...*to give light/ to give life/ to give love*...they make me miss my daughter."

"You have a daughter? "

"Yes, dear. Alice's mother is my daughter."

She sighed.

"I have not seen Mary Lynne for eight years."

"Eight years is a long time. That must be...just terrible. I'm sorry."

"Yes. It is. It's not knowing where she is...is she still alive even? I've tried to find her—hired detectives. She does not want to be found. Or she is dead. This would not surprise me, given her lifestyle. Either way, she's been dead to me for eight years now."

Amy didn't know what to say. The two women looked at each other in silence. Justine seemed so small. Amy could see the sorrow in the corners of the old woman's eyes—threatening to spill over. Without thinking she reached out and covered a withered hand with her own. Justine squeezed her fingers and the tears did spill then.

"You give me such a gift, Amelia. Thank you."

Just then, Alice peeked through one of the doorways hugging the circular room.

"Guess what?"

She skipped into the room.

Two sets of eyes followed her.

"What?"

They asked it simultaneously.

"Mrs. Lemasters has an appointment. So my studies have been cut short today. She's already given me my assignments! That means I can join the two of you for lunch!"

Oh, this child was beautiful and Amy was bewitched by those dimples.

"Lunch!"

Justine looked horrified.

"I forgot that I promised you lunch, Amelia. The poetry has given me such sweet sleep...it slipped my mind completely."

"Please don't worry about it. I usually don't eat lunch anyway."

Justine eyed her critically.

"No wonder you are so thin. Alice, your father made some of his creamy tomato soup a couple days ago. There are some cold cuts in the fridge. Will you be a dear and put us together a tray?"

The girl was thrilled. She disappeared into the galley. Amy watched the door swing behind her.

"Just...let me help."

She followed Alice into the kitchen. She found her carefully ladling soup from a tureen into three bowls. She dimpled again at Amy's presence.

"Dad won't let me use the stove when he's not home, but I'm a pro with the microwave!"

Amy opened the refrigerator door, found some ham and turkey in the bottom drawer and placed them on the tray sitting on the counter.

"The bread is over there."

Together, they created a lovely little lunch, complete with iced tea topped with mint. Amy was impressed with Alice's skill in the kitchen. *Certainly not hazardous duty*, she smiled at the thought. Maureen Doallas's poetry made for a good aperitif.

When the two returned to Justine, however, they found her sleeping.

"Let's eat in the garden, then. Shall we?"

Amy followed Alice's bobbing form through yet another door, into a solarium of sorts. There was lush greenery in the center—miniature palms and Elephant's Ear, and tropical-looking plants that lent a feel of holiday to the room. She followed Alice through sliding glass doors and into beauty.

It was a mild day for early March—the blustery wind and snow flurries of the previous week blown on to far places. The sun lit the cloudless sky like stained glass and the promise of spring was in the air. The garden was rather bare, only the crocuses brave enough to show themselves this early in the season. But Amy was taken with the hedging—the neat rows of boxwood framed them competently, lending a feel of order that Amy sorely lacked these days.

"Alice, this is beautiful!"

The girl grinned.

"Dad is teaching me about gardening. My mother used to take care of the flowers. And then Gram. But now, she's too sick, so it's up to me. I'm in charge this year."

Amy searched the child's face for any sadness at the mention of her mother. But Alice seemed quite content. She sat the tray down on a table that was strategically positioned in the shade of a small tree. The perfect hostess, she set the plates out with silverware and gestured for Amy to sit.

"Would you like to say the blessing?"

*Blessing?*

"Why don't you, Alice? You are the host, after all."

"Okay."

The child folded her hands in her lap and bowed her head.

"Thank you for this food, Lord. And thank you for sending Amy. Amen."

Alice attacked her plate with gusto. Amy was surprised at how eager she was for a bite too—something in the crisp air piqued her hunger. The soup was delicious—the perfect blend of cream, tomato, and basil. And she wondered about this Oliver—this gourmet/gardener/banker/single father who cared for the mother of his disappeared wife. She surveyed Alice under her lashes.

"How old are you, Alice?"

"I will be eleven in four months time."

Ten years old. Alice was only two when her mother left her. Amy studied the little girl.

"Daddy says he has a big surprise for me for my birthday. I was hoping he would get me a new bike. But he won't tell. Usually, he gives it away beforehand. Dad is terrible about keeping secrets! I think he almost likes to give it away…"

Amy let Alice prattle, enjoying the easy sound of her talk. They split the extra bowl of soup—the one warmed for Justine. Afterwards, Justine was still sleeping so they cleaned up together.

All the way home, Amy smiled. As she checked her mailbox before heading back inside, a realization popped.

She hadn't heard a thing from the watchers all week.

"Read it again."

Justine dipped her head and puckered her lips to the corner of the carry-out cup. The whipped cream made a mustache on her upper lip and Amy laughed. White Mocha Latte. The old woman had sighed over one just yesterday and Amy couldn't wait to surprise her with it this morning.

Justine rolled her eyes into the back of her head as she sipped.

"Oh, dear. Thank you so much for this little treat this morning, Amelia. I've always said that a good coffee makes poetry sweeter. Mmmmm."

They sipped quietly—Justine her sweet concoction and Amy her café au lait.

"Go ahead, " Justine repeated. "Read it again."

"You always want that one."

"You know I love it. But, I have a story to go with it today. I remembered it last night."

This had become their habit. Amy had been reading to Justine for four weeks now, five days a week. On the days when Justine felt well, after each poem, she would share a memory with Amy. Amy listened, sometimes asked questions, but she knew the stories were more for Justine than for her. So she let her talk as much as she wanted.

"All right then, here goes:

*What I really like*

*is how words*
*aren't needed*

*to hold in mind*

*the slant the sun takes*
*when it pitches*
*a fit*

*of rays on the sea*
*at dusk*

*or the cut-through line*
*at the horizon's edge*

*once you've pulled back*
*and turned*
*for one last look*

*at the world*

*you've traveled to*
*and through*

*to reach home."*

Amy waited. Justine took a shaky breath and set down her latte.

"I was a new bride when I first saw the sea. George's construction business was growing, but we still hadn't much money for a holiday. He rented us a small cottage on the shore and we spent a week learning the rhythm of married life from the steady beat of the Atlantic. The beaches were different then—not so busy, much quieter. We were married in March, so the tourist season had not quite started yet. My George was an athlete and every morning he would get up before the sun and swim in that cold ocean. I could barely stand to wade in the stuff, but I would wander myself awake in the surf as he swam…picking up little bits of the ocean as I waited for my new husband to finish his morning constitutional.

One morning, I sat on the cool sand waiting. The sun was beginning to show the top curve of her head—all brilliant red and orangy glow. He emerged from the water just as she started her ascension. It looked like he carried the sun on his head as he splashed toward me. And in typical George fashion, he had to get his wet all over me, reducing me to a fit of giggles right there before God and everyone."

She was quiet for a moment, lost in the memory.

"That morning I said something to George that would stick for the rest of our marriage. 'George Taylor,' I said, 'did you know the sun rises and sets on you?' And we sat together and watched her slow climb."

Justine put her coffee down on the breakfast tray at the bedside and lay back against her pillows.

"What I wouldn't give to see the ocean one more time before I die."

She studied her hands, avoiding Amy's eyes. The old woman had never shared a story about her husband before and Amy was unsure what to say.

"You must have loved him very much."

When Justine looked up, her eyes were brimming with tears.

"Yes, yes I do."

She smiled weakly and put her hand over Amy's where it rested on *Neruda's Memoirs*.

"Thank you for listening to an old woman's ramblings. You are so easy to talk to, Amelia. I never used to talk so much. But then…George has been gone for twenty-seven years now. The Lord took him far too soon. Not a day has passed that I haven't thought of him. But I am thinking of him more and more these days. I am ready to see my husband again."

She looked up with shining eyes. At the thought of losing Justine, Amy felt panic. She had only just found her. Even though it was short, their time together had filled a lacuna inside of her that she didn't know was there. She was grateful for the old woman's friendship.

Amy hesitated.

"Justine…is it certain? I mean, isn't there something the doctors can do? You don't seem so bad off to me, I mean…"

Justine patted Amy's hand.

"Oh, sweetheart, yes it is certain. I have outlived all of their predictions. I have been battling this cancer for ten years now. I've had chemo and radiation and in the beginning I wanted to fight. But it kept coming back. I'm eighty-two years old, Amelia. I'm tired. This bed is my life now. I am too weak to be moved. My bones are too fragile. I am ready for this to end."

Amy was surprised to feel tears on her cheeks. Justine lifted a gnarled finger and smoothed the wet away. Her skin was surprisingly soft on Amy's face and she cupped the younger woman's chin in her hand. Her milky eyes searched intently.

"Don't you worry about me. You need to worry about you. You have given me so much joy, Amelia. But you have much better things to do than read poetry to an old woman. You still have a whole lot of living to do."

Amy shrugged Justine's hand away and wiped her eyes.

"Do you want to hear that poem again?"

"Sure, why not? It gets better each time you read it."

So Amy read the poem again. And as she imagined the young sun ascending into the sky, aging in the slow journey across the arc of the earth, arriving at dusk with all its purples and blues— arriving home…

She knew what she had to do.

9

"Absolutely not."

He was the brick wall behind his desk and she wrestled with frustration. *Didn't he see that Justine needs this?*

"Amy, I appreciate what you want to do, but it's just not possible. We are two hours from the ocean. That may not sound long to you, but for a woman who can break a bone by simply taking a step, for a woman whose skin could be sorely compromised by sitting in a car that long, for a woman who needs nursing care every few hours…It's just too risky."

She felt heat rising to her cheeks and pursed her lips. He must think her a fool.

"Oliver, I know it's risky, but the benefits would far outweigh the danger. My ex-husband is a physician. I've already talked to him about borrowing one of the transport vans his practice uses for his surgery patients. The vans have special beds for skin management, there's even potential for an oxygen tank if necessary. I worked at his practice for ten years. I know about these things."

His eyes bored into her.

"And do you know about managing her bladder? Have you ever done a catheterization? Are you prepared to change her Depends? She lost bowel and bladder function several months ago. How do you think that will affect Justine's dignity? It's one reason she schedules you in between the nurses' visits—so you won't have to deal with that. If you traveled with Justine you would not only have to deal with it, but it may take away those few strands of pride she has left."

Amy sat still in her chair. Of course she hadn't considered these things. What was she thinking? She wanted to run from his office the way she had all those weeks ago. She felt like a little girl being chastised by a parent.

Suddenly, Oliver sprung up from his chair and turned his back to her. His wrinkled shirt flashed white in the corner of her eye. He wrapped his arms around himself—seemingly trying to calm down. She stood slowly, preparing to leave when she noticed his large frame shaking.

"Oliver?"

She took a step toward him.

He bowed his head and lifted a hand to cover his eyes. Oliver was crying. Amy remembered his hand hovering near hers that first day they met—his awkward attempt at compassion—and a wave of tenderness crashed through her composure.

She edged around the desk and tentatively placed a cool hand on his shoulder.

"It's okay. I'm sorry. I didn't realize what I was asking. I only wanted to do this for Justine."

He lifted his hand to hers and covered her small fingers with his large ones.

She edged around the desk and tentatively placed a cool hand on his shoulder.

"It's okay. I'm sorry. I didn't realize what I was asking. I only wanted to do this for Justine."

He lifted his hand to hers and for the second time in their acquaintance covered her small fingers with his large ones.

"I'm the one who is sorry."

He turned to face her, still clutching her hand.

"Justine has been…like a mother to me. She has been the

only mother Alice has known. I haven't really considered what losing her will mean—what it has meant to watch her slowly go downhill over these past months. What I wouldn't give to take her to the seashore—to see her eyes light up again. I would love to say yes, Amy. But I cannot compromise Justine's health. I don't know what I would do without her."

Amy nodded, slid her hand out of his.

"I understand. I won't mention it again. I better get going or I'll be late for our reading."

She gave him a weak smile before heading out the door.

10

She had just put the top on her peanut butter and jelly sandwich when there came a light knock. She glanced at the clock. Who would come calling to her house at dinner time? She briefly entertained the thought of ignoring it, but the tapping came again—more insistent this time. She reluctantly set the sandwich down and went to the front door.

She opened it just a crack, only to have it pushed in from the outside at the slight give.

"Alice!"

"Dad said to come get you, Amy. You're invited to dinner."

Amy didn't know what to say. Alice was smiling like she had a secret.

"Well…I just made a sandwich…"

"You have to come! Gram will be so disappointed if you don't."

Feeling slightly coerced, Amy grabbed a sweater and Alice's hand and they walked down the street to the gated house together.

"What is this all about?" She glanced over at the girl.

"You'll see…"

That mischievous smile again.

When they entered the house, it was eerily quiet. Alice led her down the hall, through the Great Room, through the sun room, and out the garden doors.

Amy drew breath sharply at what she saw.

The entire garden courtyard had been turned into a beach.

The grass and stone were covered with sand. There was a large mural of an ocean scene somehow hung along the south wall. A tiki bar with coconuts hanging from a grass umbrella sat in the corner. Island music drifted from speakers.

And there was Justine, in the middle of it all, sitting in a wheelchair. Grinning from ear to ear.

"Welcome to the beach, " she said, as Amy looked around in wonder. Oliver appeared from somewhere and put a lei around her neck. He smiled down at her.

"What do you think?"

She was speechless.

11

The moon was slowly rising over the poster board horizon— its waxing gibbous a face turned away from their party. Amy wiggled her toes in the cool sand. Justine leaned in close.

*"This has all been so…re-enchanting."*

She dimpled and Amy realized just how strongly Alice resembled her grandmother. She returned Justine's smile. She knew the poem her friend referred to. It was Maureen's "To Be Re-enchanted is Uneasy." She gave her the favorite verse.

> *"I would as soon die as miss*
> *morning coming up, the swelling round*
> *of cloud before lightbursts, the press*
> *of stars to complete a night's worth of sky*
> *for clearing dreams…"*

Justine leaned back in her chair and looked up at the midnight blue.

*"The press of stars to complete a night's worth of sky…*Oh, that's nice."

She sighed deep.

"Oh, but I fear I will have to miss morning coming up. I will settle for these stars pressing in and ready for the dreamland. Oliver, will you help me to bed? This has been such a wonderful evening. I don't want to spoil it by staying up too late. I am tired. Such a good tired, though."

They had pulled the chairs up to the firepit and Oliver and Alice were cuddled in the glider–Oliver's arms making a warm nest for his girl. Though spring had announced its arrival by way of bloom on nearby hills, the evenings were still cool and the clear sky lent a nip to the air. Amy was thankful for her sweater and drew a bit closer to the fire as the others began to stir.

"Alice, you should be getting ready for bed too, sweetheart."

Oliver disentangled himself from the gangly arms of a ten year old.

"But, dad! I'm not tired! Let me stay up a little bit longer, please?"

Oliver looked at a loss, so Amy attempted a rescue.

"I should be going too. Alice, it is getting late. Maybe you should listen to your dad."

Alice's lip curled.

"May I stay up just long enough for you to get Gram settled, Dad? Amy can keep me company, can't you?"

She turned those blue eyes on Amy and resistance was futile.

"Sure, I can. But as soon as your dad gets back...I have to go, okay?"

"Oh, all right."

Amy bent to give Justine a goodnight hug. She was surprised to have a papery kiss planted on her cheek.

"Thank you, Amelia." There were tears in the old woman's eyes. "I couldn't have asked for a nicer evening."

As Oliver wheeled her away, Amy nestled into the glider beside Alice. The girl leaned into Amy and she wrapped arms around the skinny frame. They rocked back and forth, quiet—watching the fire die down and listening to its soft burn. Amy could feel Alice giving in to sleep, feel the small body relax in her arms. She buried her face in the girl's hair and felt her heart leap. Alice smelled like sunscreen and grape popsicle and the scent of her was causing Amy's heart to break.

"This has been the best night, " Alice murmured.

"Yes, " Amy said, staring into the fire. "It has."

"Like having a real family."

Amy hugged her tighter—felt the pain of those few words and they rocked steady. They were one, and she knew the precise moment that sleep came because Alice's breathing slowed and the girl's body rested heavy against her own.

"Is she asleep?"

Oliver sat in the lawn chair beside the glider and held his hands to the fire.

"I think so. Only just."

"Maybe you should sit a little bit. Just to make sure she is in a good deep sleep before I carry her up."

Something about his smile made Amy blush. She was thankful for the settling dark.

"Thank you for inviting me tonight. It was…really nice."

"I couldn't *not* invite you. It was your idea, after all."

"This?" She gestured around the garden. "This wasn't my idea! How in the world did you do it all?"

He grinned wider, poked the fire with one of the sticks they had used to roast the marshmallows earlier.

"Justine still has a lot of friends in the construction business, you know. That was what George did. Owned a huge construction company. The guys who bought it from her after he died were with him forever. They are crazy about Justine. Would do anything for her. So, I just…made a few phone calls."

"Well, it's amazing. I'm re-enchanted too."

"I'm glad."

He looked away.

"Thank you for everything you do, Amy. Alice is just crazy about you and Justine…I've seen new hope in her these past weeks."

"All I do is give her poetry."

"And that means everything. All the poetry has been gone from her life for a long time."

He looked up and into Amy's eyes.

"And from mine too."

Something inside of her felt like it would break if he kept looking at her like that and fear came calling. The watchers can never resist the call of fear.

But Oliver's next words put the stopper on the voices of her old enemies and sent Amy's heart spinning.

12

"Do you want to move in with us?"

"Excuse me?"

He shifted uncomfortably in his seat and flashed her a crooked smile.

"It was Justine's idea. She thought it might be a way we could help each other out. Right now, she is unable to do so much for Alice. Alice is alone so much these days. She adores you, Amy. We just thought…until you get back on your feet…and since you aren't working right now…"

"That I would have nothing better to do?"

The watchers started laughing in her head and she put her fingers to her temples. The anger was their trademark and she fought hard to control her emotions. Oliver looked stunned.

"No, Amy. That's not what I meant. Justine mentioned you are having some financial concerns. She said she thought you needed some healing time before going back to work full time. She only wants to help. And it would be invaluable help to us. Of course, we would pay you very well, I know we're asking you to give up a lot…"

Amy eased Alice out of her arms and slid the sleeping child onto the glider. Something caught inside her, but she turned and grabbed the book off the table.

"I have to go."

Oliver stood up beside her.

"Amy, please…"

She moved toward the door. He followed.

"At least let me walk you home after I put Alice into her bed, I feel so horrible. This didn't go the way I planned…"

"I'm fine. I know my way home."

He put his hand on her arm and she shrugged it off, whirling around to face him.

"Look, Oliver, I'm not for sale. Nor am I some kind of social project to entertain your family. I am a woman who is try-ing to put her life back together. This may be hard for you to believe, but at one time, I was quite successful. I'm very good at what I do. I just haven't found the right opportunity, I just…"

She was shaking. He put his hand back on her arm.

"I know all this, Amy. Did you forget I've seen your vitae? I had never been more impressed by a candidate before you came into my office. Justine just thought you needed some time…"

"I'm fine! Would you please tell Justine to mind her own business? I need a real job to pick up the pieces of my life, not some glorified babysitting position."

She saw the words hit him and he flinched. Even as she said them, she knew she didn't mean them. She had grown to love Justine and Alice. The hurtful words came from the watchers.

They stared at each other, her icy blue locked with his steel gray. Finally, he looked down.

"I guess there's nothing more to say then."

She cried on the short walk home, berating the voices in her head, berating herself.

"Why? Why did I say those things?"

She stumbled into her living room and dropped onto the couch. She stared at the ceiling, tears leaking out the corners of her eyes leaving wet tracks down her cheeks.

"Why do I always ruin everything?"

13

She must have fallen asleep because the pounding came at 3 a.m. to wake her.

"What?" she mumbled in her half sleep. She could hear someone pounding on the door. *Really? Was someone pounding on her door at 3 a.m.?* She sat bolt upright. Fear seized her and she crept through the hallway to the front of the small living quarters. She peeked through the sidelight.

It was Oliver.

She flung the door open.

"Oliver, what in the world?"

"I'm sorry to come at this hour. I wouldn't, you know I wouldn't. It's Justine. She's had a seizure. She's in terrible pain. She won't let me take her to the hospital, Amy. She's asking for you. And that damn book. I don't know what to do. She's in terrible pain…"

The panic and helplessness in his voice shed any remnant of sleep left in her body. She ran into the living room and grabbed *Neruda's Memoirs* off the couch and flew back to him and out the door.

"Come on."

~

She could hear Justine's loud moans as soon as they walked through the door. She ran to her, clutching *Neruda's Memoirs* tightly to her chest. Alice was at her grandmother's side, face streaked and pinched.

"Alice, what are you doing out of bed?"

Oliver's voice was filled with agony.

"Daddy? Daddy, please help her! I can't help her, Daddy. I've tried everything."

He went to her and wrapped his arms around her. Alice sobbed into his chest.

Amy cautiously approached the bedside. Justine's body arched in pain and she cried out. Her whole body shook with sobs.

"Oh, God, make it stop! Oh, God, oh, God, oh God…"

Amy recognized a prayer in Justine's pleas. She said nothing by way of greeting; just fell right into the words.

### *'Trial Season*

*Only yesterday did earth redress*
*its layers of browned forgotten bloom*

*shedding its sheath for winter with the pace*
*of an old man making do with a gimp left leg…"*

Justine turned empty eyes on Amy. She squinted in concentration, vacancy flickered.

"Amy?"

Amy leaned over the bed and grasped Justine's hand.

"Yes, it's me. I'm here, Justine. I'm here."

A pain gripped the old woman and her back arched again in response to the violent conversation taking place in her body. She screamed.

"Oh, God. "

She searched Amy's face, struggling to maintain recognition.
"Help me."

Amy reached up and smoothed her friend's brow. Over and over she caressed her face and hair.

"Shhhh. It's okay. I'm here. I'm not leaving."

"The words…"

Amy scrambled to open the book again.

*"Things happen.*

*Spring starts up*
*a widespread yellow operation*

*braced for the challenge,*
*armed with emerald swords…"*

She read on. She was vaguely conscious of Oliver and Alice shifting noiselessly on the settee. She paid no mind. Only read the words until Justine's body was still and quiet. Finally giving in to the magic of poetry.

14

Oliver called hospice the next day. The nurses came and went like ghosts—helping Justine with pain management and soothing the rest of them with knowing words. Amy was shocked at the sudden deterioration in her friend. She brought a bag of clothes and moved them in to a spare bedroom. "Just for now," she told Oliver, who simply hugged her. He moved a cot into the living room for her after finding her on the couch nearest Justine that first morning.

Moments of lucidity were scarce and Amy grieved quietly the loss. Most often, Justine mistook Amy for her daughter, which Amy found unsettling.

"I love you, Mary Lynne, " she said one day. She gripped Amy's hand with untold strength and stared fiercely into her eyes. "Don't you ever forget that, okay?"

Amy stared into those milky eyes and felt her insides melt like sugar in water.

"I love you too, mama, " she said.

She knew it was right to do, by the peace that settled over Justine's face. She lifted her hand and smoothed the old woman's hair back from her brow.

"I love you so much."

She continued to read the poems to Justine's limp figure. And though it seemed a pointless task, Amy noticed that during the reading, her friend slept less restlessly. Amy whispered the words deep into the night, grateful for the way they calmed her too.

Alice was another story. The girl had taken to insomnia, and often Amy would wake up in the wee hours to find her standing over her grandmother, still and watching. She said nothing to the child at first, knowing the way fear can gnaw away at the insides. Alice's world was about to change.

Amy awoke one night to the sound of muffled sobs. She found Alice on the couch, a crumpled ball of a girl.

"Alice?"

The sniffing slowed to a drip.

"Alice, honey?"

The girl padded over to Amy's cot. Amy said nothing, just lifted the blanket and let her climb on in. She wrapped herself around that bundle of sadness, willing her arms to be strength enough for them both. She slept better than she had for days and she thought Alice did too. In the morning, she was aware of a shadow standing over them. She opened her eyes to Oliver's. His were soft from looking at his daughter in sleep, but she saw something else there too. Was it…fear? Grief? Maybe both she decided.

"You okay?"

She nodded.

"Call me if you need me, okay?"

She nodded again. He turned to leave but stopped. Slowly he turned back around, kneeled beside the cot and kissed Alice's forehead. Then he searched out Amy's hand under the covers and lifted it to his lips too. His eyes were glistening and he spoke without looking at her.

"These are your best parts, Amy. These pieces of you… you were right, that first time we met. Can't put this on a resume. For what you give…I am so grateful."

The last was said in a whisper. And then he was gone. Amy lifted her hand to her face. It smelled of him. She slowly inhaled and fell back to sleep, with his daughter breathing softly beside her.

15

"Alice! Do hurry or we'll be late!"

Amy called down the corridor, trying not to be annoyed. She glanced in the foyer mirror, eyeing her hair critically between the reflection of bits of the flower arrangement on the hall table.

"Alice! Oh!"

The girl glided through the arched doorway. The only thing on her face was that dimpled smile that always melted Amy's heart—and a little lip gloss. Alice had just turned fifteen last week and Amy swallowed hard at how grown up she looked in taffeta and pearls.

"Oh, honey. You are *so* beautiful."

Alice curtsied and spun around slowly so Amy could appreciate the effect of the softly billowing skirt.

"And you are going to knock dad's socks off!"

Amy had chosen a more sedate outfit—a long straight silk in a peachy color. She did feel pretty–despite her nervousness–and she couldn't help smiling at Alice's enthusiasm. They didn't get to dress up like this often.

"Are you ready? We'd better get going. Don't want to keep the governor waiting."

She winked at Alice.

"Do you have your book?"

Alice nodded, lifting her bag in response as they hurried out the door.

Five years. That's how long it had taken. The cancer center had been operating now for almost a year, but tonight marked the official completion of phase one of the project. Justine's project.

Amy and Oliver had both been surprised by the thought and detail the old woman had put into the planning. Her will was very meticulous, but much of her plan was already well underway when she passed. The land had already been purchased, the architect consulted, and preliminary discussions initiated with St. Joe's. It had taken some doing, but when Oliver had secured the partnership with the medical school, it was just a matter of building the thing. And Justine had even arranged that—contracting her husband's former company to handle it all.

Tonight, they would celebrate. She felt her pulse quicken a bit as she pulled up to the breezeway. Before the valet could open the door she glanced over at her stepdaughter.

"Are you ready for this?"

Alice dimpled again.

"Sure I am. It's all for Gram. It'll be grand."

And it was grand. The concourse of the center had been turned into a ballroom for the evening. The floors gleamed and the chandelier partialed out twinkling light. Circular tables were peppered here and there for the esteemed guests who would arrive later. Amy's heels clicked sharply on the brightly waxed floor as she approached the small group of figures gathered near the podium. Oliver broke from the group as she drew near and extended his hand to take hers.

She felt herself relax as he gently folded her in his arms.

"You look stunning."

He whispered in her ear and his breath sent shivers down her neck. How did he always do that? She smiled up at him and he reached his other arm out to gather Alice to him.

"Ladies and Gentleman, we may begin the ceremony.

The driving forces behind the George and Justine Taylor Cancer Center have arrived."

There were so many names that Amy lost track. The governor said "a few words" behind the podium and the senator from the fourth district was not to be left out. Her face felt like it would break from the smiling. But soon, she and Alice cut the ribbon—posing numerous times for the newspaper photographers—and she was free to sit. She glanced at her watch. The dinner would begin in half an hour. She sidled up to Oliver, who was hobnobbing with some suits, and leaned close to his ear.

"Can you hold down the fort for a wee bit?"

He glanced knowingly at the book she held in her hands.

"If I must…"

It was all she needed to hear. She found Alice and they slipped down the back corridor, up the elevator and clicked heels down the shiny second floor hallway. Amy smiled as they passed the colorful murals. When they reached the nurses' station, the white-clad figures smiled and nodded, but continued their work without interruption. Alice hurried to the common room but Amy lingered in the large arch of the doorway.

"Alice!"

She watched as the children gathered around her girl, grinning from ear to ear. These little ones had been here so long they had gotten to know Alice quite well. How they loved her. Such a mix of joy and sadness—their shiny round heads bowed into Alice's. The tiniest ones clamored for a turn on her lap as their parents smiled them on nearby.

"You look like a princess, " one of them offered in awe-filled tones.

Alice laughed and pulled out her book.

"Who's ready for some poetry?"

A collective cheer rose and soon the room was hushed of all but Alice's rhythmic tones.

It never ceased to amaze Amy how even the youngest was spellbound at the reading. She thought of Justine's last days, felt a tiny twist in her heart.

*I miss you, my friend.*

She fingered the two volumes in her hands and turned her back on the sweet scene of poetry. There was someone she needed to see.

The south wing was quiet this evening and Amy was conscious of the approaching dark. She nodded to the nurses at the desk and slipped into room 204.

"Emory?"

She knocked lightly on the door as she entered.

There was no response, but as she drew near his bedside, he stirred.

"Who is it?"

She put her warm hand over his fingers.

"Amy?"

His vision had left him long ago but his other senses were as sharp as the north star on a clear night.

"Yes, it's me."

"I was wondering what was taking you so long tonight."

"Tonight is the dinner, remember? That ceremony I told you about? I'm sorry I'm a bit later than usual."

"Did you bring it? The book?"

"Yes, I did."

"Will you read me the one? My favorite? I feel the need."

She made no reply, just opened the book to the familiar words.

> *"No Easy Solace*
>
> *No easy solace*
> *comes*
>
> *by treasure*
> *both moth and rust consume.*
>
> *The heart contused,*
> *it gives no solace*
>
> *to memory once blacked*
> *and blued.*
>
> *Love*
> *its light from star or moon*
>
> *crocheted*
> *as from a spider's womb."*

After the reading, she wiped the tears from his eyes as she always did and he sighed and they were quiet. He was in a mood tonight and she couldn't wait for him this time.

"Emory?"

He sighed at the breaking of the hush—though he knew her nature by now and fully expected it.

"Yes?"

"I have a surprise for you. It's a new book. We've read through *Neruda's Memoirs* so many times now…I thought you might enjoy something new. It's called *Delicate Machinery Suspended.* It's by a poet who is new to me—Anne M. Doe Overstreet. I think you'll like it…she's very…well, she notices things."

He was quiet. Amy sat in stilled silence, afraid to breathe.

When he finally spoke it was with a gruff vulnerability.

"You're not to leave *Neruda's Memoirs* behind when you come, you hear?"

"No, of course not, I know it's your favorite. I just thought…"

"Well, then. Read, girl. Read. Let's see what this Overstreet poet has to offer."

Amy smiled in the dim light. She was going to be late for the dinner. And she didn't care one bit.

# Also From T. S. Poetry Press

*How to Read a Poem: Based on the Billy Collins Poem "Introduction to Poetry,"* by Tania Runyan

No reader, experienced or new to reading poems, will want to miss this winsome and surprising way into the rich, wonderful conversations that poetry makes possible.

—David Wright, Assistant Professor of English at Monmouth College, IL

*The Joy of Poetry: How to Keep, Save & Make Your Life With Poems,* by Megan Willome

This book is many things. An unpretentious, funny, and poignant memoir; a defense of poetry; and a response to literature that has touched her life. It's also the story of a daughter who loses her mother to cancer. The author links these things into a narrative much like that of a novel. I loved this book. As soon as I finished, I began reading it again.

—David Lee Garrison, author of *Playing Bach in the D. C. Metro*